For Jeanne
For Pia

Originally published in France by Editions du Seuil in 1999 under the title Maman était petite avant d'être grande.

Copyright © 1999 by Editions du Seuil.

Original ISBN 2-02-033512-3.

English translation © 2003 by Editions du Seuil.

Barbie is a registered trademark of Mattel, Inc.

Manufactured in Italy.

Library of Congress Cataloging-in-Publication Data
Larrondo, Valerie.
[Maman était petite avant d'être grande. English]
When Mommy was little / Valerie Larrondo ; Claudine Desmarteau.
p. cm.
Summary: It seems that Mommy may not have always been the well-behaved
little girl she claims to have been.
ISBN 2-02-059693-8
[1. Mothers–Fiction. 2. Behavior–Fiction.] I. Desmarteau, Claudine.
II. Title.
PZ7.L32378Wh 2003
[E]– dc21
2002156746

Distributed in Canada by Raincoast Books
9050 Shaughnessy Street, Vancouver, British Columbia V6P 6E5

10 9 8 7 6 5 4 3 2 1

Chronicle Books LLC
85 Second Street, San Francisco, California 94105

www.chroniclekids.com

Valérie Larrondo   Claudine Desmarteau

WHEN MOMMY WAS LITTLE

seuil ᴏᴏ chronicle

See this picture?

This is my mommy

when she was little.

My mommy says

that when she was little,

she ate everything

on her plate.

She never

put her fingers

in her nose.

She never pulled

the dog's tail.

She never played doctor

with the little boy

next door.

She NEVER

used rude words.

POOP FART PEEPEE FART PEEPEE POOP
PEEPEE FART POOP FART PEEPEE
FART PEEPEE POOP PEEPEE FART POOP
POOP
FART
PEEPEE

She always brushed her teeth,

combed her hair,

said goodnight to her mom and dad,

went to bed and fell asleep right away,

without calling out,

without asking for a drink,

or another story,

or saying she had a tummyache,

or she had to go to the bathroom...again!

MOMMY

THIRSTY

SCARED

STORY

DADDY

POTTY

Mommy never drew on the wall with

permanent markers.

She was always polite,

especially to old ladies.

Excuse me, ma'am, I'm sorry to bother you, but you seem to have a big hairy wart on your chin.

Mommy never played

with her mother's

makeup.*

* Except when she really had to.

Mommy never got angry.

She never demanded

a Barbie.

Mommy was always sweet to her parents.

Both of them.

She never talked back.

In fact, sometimes

she didn't talk at all.

She loved

to read her little brother

to sleep.

She was never jealous of him.
In fact, she always gave him compliments.

Mommy

was always careful

with other children's toys.

Mommy never behaved like a little monster.

And I always believe

every word

my mommy says.

Don't you?